For Elliott and Clara and their clever
mommy, Amy, a good reader and an
excellent rhymer. —K.N.

This book is especially for the constantly
smiley, giggly, wonderful Ryan. —D.W.

Farrar Straus Giroux Books for Young Readers
An imprint of Macmillan Publishing Group, LLC
120 Broadway, New York, NY 10271 • mackids.com

Our books may be purchased in bulk for promotional, educational, or business use. Please contact your
local bookseller or the Macmillan Corporate and Premium Sales Department at (800) 221-7945 ext. 5442
or by email at MacmillanSpecialMarkets@macmillan.com.

Library of Congress Control Number: 2022013804

First edition, 2023
Book design by Aram Kim and Gene Vosough
Color separations by Bright Arts (H.K.) Ltd.
Printed in China by Toppan Leefung Printing Ltd., Dongguan City, Guangdong Province

ISBN 978-0-374-38904-8 (hardcover)
1 3 5 7 9 10 8 6 4 2

THE
BEARS
SHARED

Kim Norman Pictures by David Walker

Farrar Straus Giroux

New York

This is the lair the bears shared.

This is the hair that came
from the lair
the bears shared.

This is the bird that borrowed the hair
that came from the lair
the bears shared.

This is the nest built by the bird
that borrowed the hair
that came from the lair
the bears shared.

This is the tree, tall as can be,
that held the nest
built by the bird
that borrowed the hair
that came from the lair
the bears shared.

This is the wind that howled from the west
that shook up the tree that sheltered the nest,
the cozy nest,
and the mama bird
that borrowed the hair
that came from the lair
the bears shared.

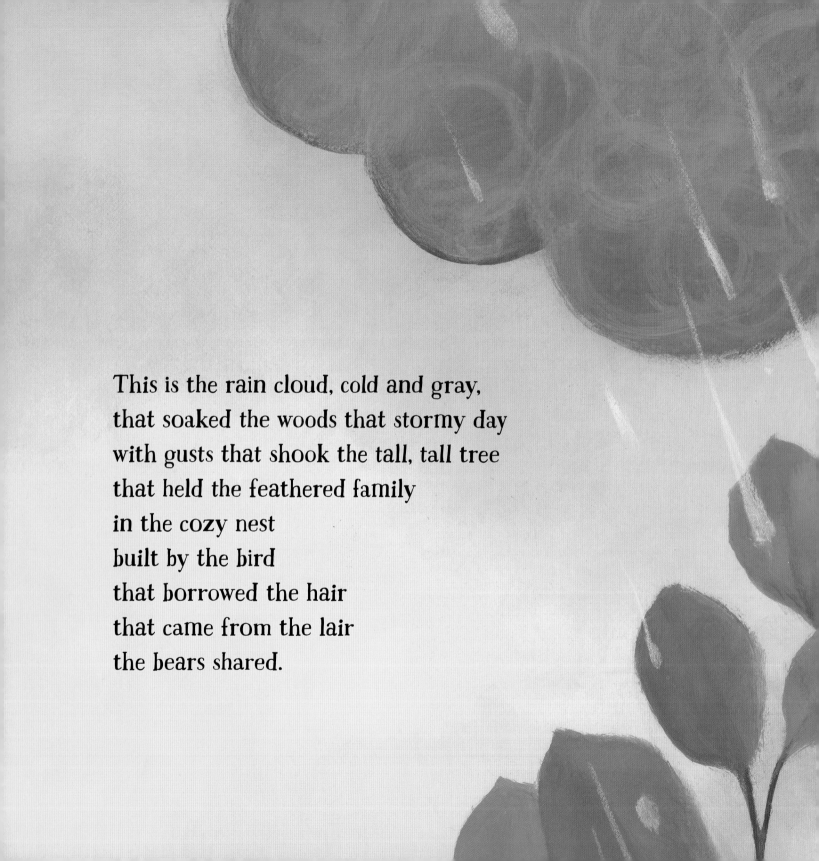

This is the rain cloud, cold and gray,
that soaked the woods that stormy day
with gusts that shook the tall, tall tree
that held the feathered family
in the cozy nest
built by the bird
that borrowed the hair
that came from the lair
the bears shared.

This is the *CRACK!* of the tall, tall tree
that thrashed its branches frightfully

as water whirled on wind from the west,
a wind that scooped up bird and nest
and hair that smelled like drizzly bear
that scattered in the snapping air,
the air outside the open lair
the bears shared.

This is the bush with bouncy boughs
that caught the birds while brown bears drowsed.
The babies landed, chirpingly,
upon its branches—

one,

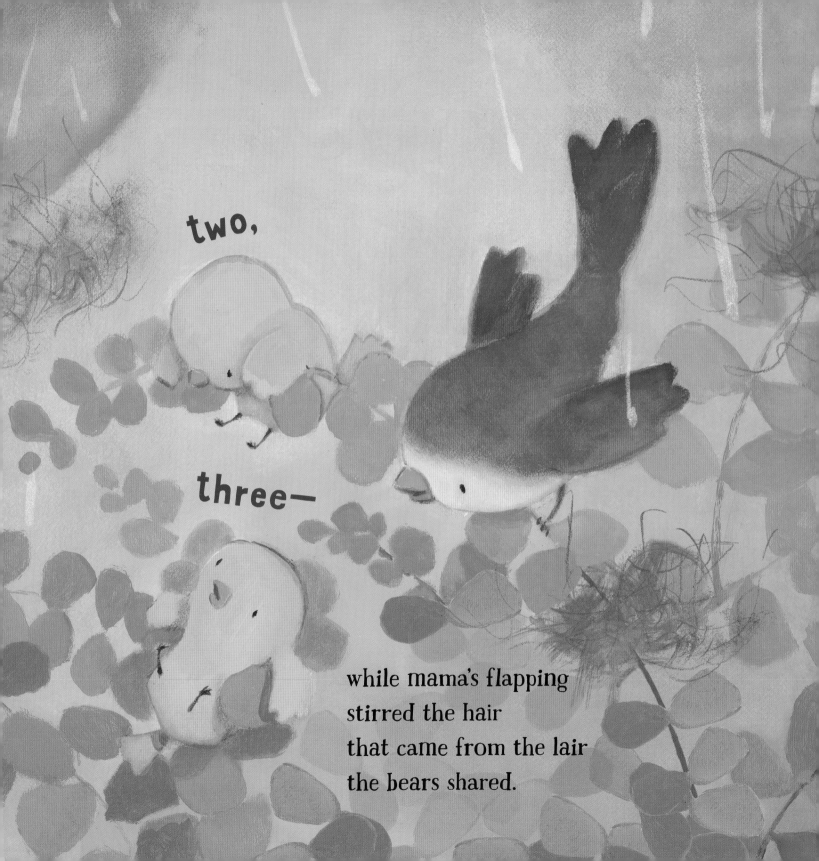

two,

three—

while mama's flapping
stirred the hair
that came from the lair
the bears shared.

This is the entrance, now a slide,
that gave the birds a muddy ride.
They flitted, flipped, and slipped inside
the hairy lair
the bears shared.

This is the snort of groggy bears
that slept through storms and borrowed hairs.
But startled from their comfy sleep
by frantic chimes of "Cheep! Cheep! Cheep!"
their bleary eyes could only stare
as feathers fanned the beary air
that came from the lair
the bears shared.

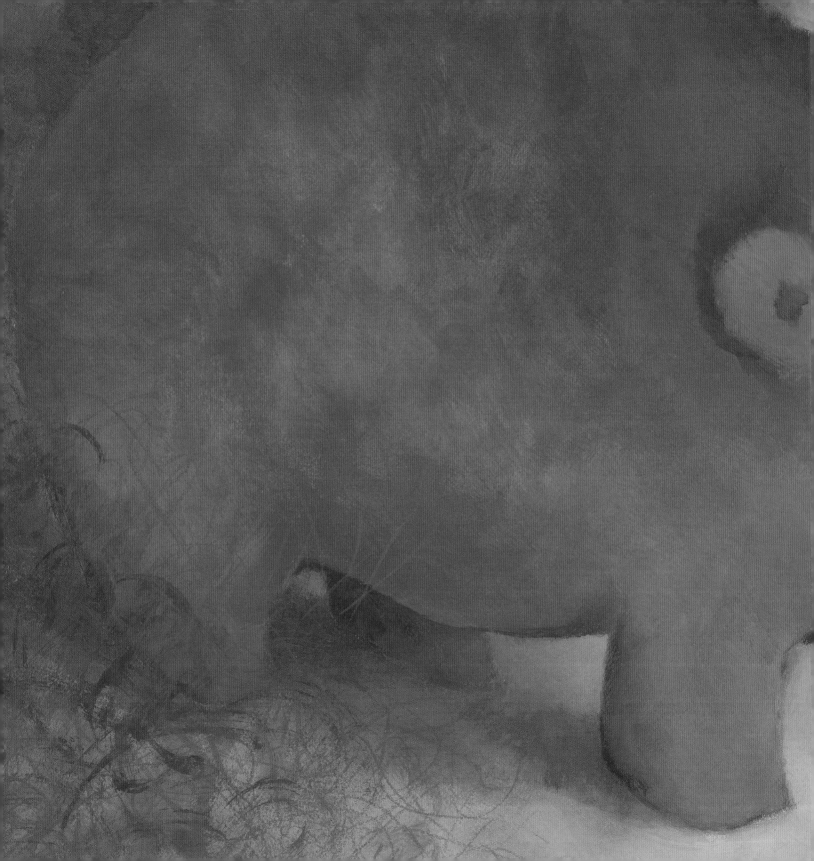

This is the moment,
beak to snout,
the mothers checked
each other out,

while big-eyed babies, scrawny things,
protected by a pair of wings,
and furry babies, brown and plump,
peered out, behind a rounded rump
that weeks ago had shed the hair
that came from the lair
the bears shared.

This is the hush within the storm
that made the room feel whisper warm
for bird and bear
with love to spare . . .

that filled the lair
the bears shared.

Author's Note

Birds make great neighbors. Because many of them eat insects, they can help make your house and yard a better place for YOU. Large hunting birds like hawks and owls help keep rodents like mice and rats away. Sometimes they even catch snakes!

Tiny birds such as hummingbirds and orioles sip a sugary liquid, called "nectar," from the flowers. Moving from blossom to blossom, birds spread pollen from one flower to another. This will produce more flowers, which means even more birds will visit the flowers to spread pollen *again*. It's a sweet, colorful circle of bird life!

Want to taste nectar, too? In spring and early summer, look for honeysuckle vines with white or yellow flowers shaped like tiny trumpets. Pluck a blossom and pinch the base of the flower. Now gently pull out the long stamen attached to the end. As the stamen passes through the flower, nectar will come with it, forming a tiny bead of sweet liquid you can touch to your tongue. Be sure to ask an adult first, to make certain it really is a safe-to-eat honeysuckle plant. (The leaves are also safe, but they don't taste very good.)

Humans can be good neighbors to birds, too. The more "bird-friendly" the yard, the more birds that will want to live there. Besides flowers, humans can grow fruits like wild grape vines or berry bushes. Birds also enjoy larger fruit. Apples, plums, and pears grow on trees that blossom beautifully in spring and shade the yard in summer.

If you want to be a *really* good friend to your avian neighbors ("avian" means anything related to birds), you can supply materials for their nests. Birds build nests from all kinds of things, from leaves and twigs to grass, pebbles, and their own feathers! They also like to use objects we might think of as trash, like short bits of yarn, broken broom straws, and old spiderwebs.